THE STORY OF DIEGO IN SAINT AUGUSTINE 1684

Richard B. Christie

This book is dedicated to my friend and fellow Historical reenactor for his help with the Spanish language translation.

Orlando Ramirez

(Don Orlando Fernando Sancho Ramírez
de Arellano Rodríguez-Montalvo
de Velázquez-Irizarry Carlo II.)

Writers' Branding
(877) 608-6550
www.writersbranding.com
media@writersbranding.com

CONTENTS

<u>Forward</u>

The following pages represent a fictional story that describes the day-to-day life of a small family living in the second half of the seventeenth century in the city of Saint Augustine, Florida.

Although references to specific historical events are factual, the characters' actions and statements are from the author's imagination and do not represent actual facts.

There are areas where historical information has come from unknown sources or multiple unidentified sources.

With this in mind, all contributions from both known and unknown sources are very much appreciated and acknowledged.

It is with additional appreciation that knowledge from the referenced time period is provided through the efforts of many volunteer reenactors who, together with the author, try to bring history alive for the many visitors who come to the oldest continuously occupied city in America, Saint Augustine, Florida.

PROLOGUE
MAY 28,1668

Pedro Rivera could not sleep. For some reason, he had awakened and then got out of bed to listen again for the sound he thought he had heard. It was very dark outside, and still about four hours before first light, but there was moonlight, and the glow was enough for him to move about in his small cottage without waking his wife Maria or his son Diego.

He began to think he had imagined it, when he again heard, in the distance, several musket shots and someone yelling. It was too far away for him to listen to what was being said, but there was a tone of fear that stirred alarm.

For one hundred and three years, the small remote village of Saint Augustine, in the northern reach of Spanish Florida, had grown from a small military outpost into a thriving little town. Although far from the Spanish-controlled Caribbean cities, they were in a good position, close enough to the northern border, to keep out potential British intervention into the Spanish claimed territory of La Florida.

Although its economy was growing, many of the town's everyday needs were still supplied by the Spanish ships that would sail north along the eastern coast of the La Florida peninsula. Food supplies of flour, grains, and various other items needed for this remote town would occasionally be shipped from Veracruz, Mexico, and several Spanish-controlled Caribbean islands.

Although shipments of these and other various items are usually requested, reliable communications between Saint Augustine and the big cities in the Caribbean were not always available. A delivery, however, was currently due with a cargo of much-needed grains and flour; but it had fallen several days behind its scheduled arrival.

Weather conditions were fair, so with concern, the Presidio of Saint Augustine had dispatched their own small Frigate with instructions to sail south and try to find the overdue ship and its cargo.

Late in the afternoon of May 28, 1668, two northbound ships were sighted off the southern coast. It soon became apparent that those ships were, indeed, the vessels they expected, since one of them was their own Frigate; but they would arrive too late to be disembarking today. So, they would anchor offshore and wait until morning.

It was with relief that Don Francisco de la Guerra y de la Vega, the Governor of La Florida, ordered the garrison soldiers to rack their matchlock muskets at the guardhouse, about a quarter mile from the city's fort, and go home to sleep.

As he did many nights, Cabo (Corporal) Miguel de Monzon had left his home late that evening and had gone fishing, in his dugout canoe.

At about 1:00 a.m., he heard the sound of many oars pulling across the water, and in the darkness, he quickly realized that it was not good for so many longboats to be shore bound at that hour and moved to sound the alarm. As he began rowing toward the town wharf, the corsairs raced after him and shot him twice as he reached the shore.

Although wounded, Monzon began shouting a belated warning and managed to reach the safety of the city's decaying wooden fortress. Behind him, the buccaneers stormed ashore.

It was probably those musket shots and Cabo Monzon's yells that had awakened Pedro, and now he could hear additional shrieks and noise.

The townspeople were caught entirely by surprise as groups of pirates rushed through the streets, yelling, and frequently seizing or shooting the frightened, sleepy inhabitants as they emerged from their homes.

As government officials also heard the noise and realized what was happening, the senior officer of the presidio's garrison, Sergeant Major Nicolas Ponce de

Leon, quickly rushed to the guardhouse only to find it had already been searched and deserted.

As the roving groups of pirates were forming over at the fort ready to rush into it, the Sergeant Major was able to assemble and guide over a hundred bewildered men, women, children, and even some unarmed soldiers, to safety in the woods about a league away.

Pedro, after hearing the yelling from two streets away, then, hearing muskets firing, realized the town was under siege. From the bed in the corner room of their small cottage, he listened to his wife Maria say: "Pedro, what is happening?"

He answered: "Get dressed for woods travel quickly, and make sure Diego also is dressed for the woods; I believe we need to escape from an attack."

As Maria called to Diego and they struggled to get dressed, Pedro grabbed his matchlock musket and, as he slid the 'twelve-apostles' powder belt over his shoulder, turned to the door and heard yells from several of their neighbors also preparing to run and hide.

It was then that he heard Sergeant Major Nicolas Ponce de Leon yelling to those nearby residents to follow his lead to the woods and safety.

Turning to Maria and his six-year-old son Diego, he said: "Go, Maria, follow the 'Sargento' into the woods, I will stay and help defend our home."

Maria, knowing her husband, could not say anything to change his mind; so, she threw her arms around him one more time, took Diego by the hand, and fled out the door to escape with so many other women and children.

Pedro stood and watched them disappear into the pines and palms that surrounded their home until he could no longer see them. He turned to the crucifix on the wall, fell to his knees, and prayed they and their town would survive.

A pounding at the door revealed seven of his neighbors, all dressed as he was with weapons and powder ready to defend their town. He quickly joined their ranks, and they spread out around whatever defensive barriers they could find and took aim at the pirates as they came rushing down the street.

As other raiders crossed the city's plaza and entered the Government House, Governor Francisco de la Guerra y de la Vega had seen them approaching and knew he had to get out and over to the fort. He must defend it, for it was one of his primary duties as Governor.

A hidden door was his escape, and, with the pirates following him close on his heels, he reached the fort's enclosure along with several other refugees. Those at the fort were already alerted by the noise of musket fire, yelling, and screams of fear.

When notified of the raid, the lieutenant at the fort, Captain Mateo Pacheco Salgado, alerted the troops on duty. They opened the enclosure's gate to admit the Governor and other royal officials, and a handful of additional men. The Governor immediately took command of the thirty-three available men.

The stockade was old and dilapidated, with wooden walls and decks, but it gave them the high ground for defense. The Governor immediately ordered open the powder magazine and distributed ammunition to those soldiers who were present, but before the cannons could be loaded, the pirates attacked the fortress.

The corsairs repeatedly tried to storm the walls for the next hour and a half, only to be driven back by heavy musket fire. The buccaneers finally withdrew, with eleven of their men dead and nineteen wounded.

Further south in town, the citizen militia that included Pedro Rivera was overwhelmed by the sheer numbers of pirates and their ruthless desire to sack every house and building.

As two of those brigands came running at the men Pedro and his neighbor Carlos, both fired at the same time and watched them fall, as the musket balls hit both in the middle of their chests.

Both men stood up to reload, and then, at the same time, they too were hit by musket fire, but this time it was from pirates charging in from the other side. Death was quick, and both Pedro and Carlos fell to the ground on top of their muskets.

They would never know it, but with daylight came another vessel. It was the pirate Captain Robert Searle's own ship, the sixty-ton 'Cagway.' It arrived and anchored in the bay alongside the other two vessels.

The Veracruz ship had been taken at sea a few days earlier, and when the Presidio's Frigate appeared, it also was captured at sea. Both ships were then sailed to Saint Augustine by the pirates, and they now were anchored in the bay.

After the late nighttime attack on the shore, the corsairs returned to complete the sacking of Saint Augustine in daylight. Even the parish church and the Franciscan convent chapels were not left alone, and they too would lose all their ornaments.

Houses were searched and robbed of jewels and other valuables. The booty was transported to, and loaded aboard, the Cagway, and the ship from Veracruz.

It would be several days before those who had survived in the woods could return to the carnage that had been their homes. There were many dead bodies still lying in the street, and the odor was appalling.

Together with many of their neighbors, Maria and Diego returned to the devastation and began the task of finding their dead family members and see to proper burials as best they could.

Six-year-old Diego grew ten years in his mind, if not his body, when he saw his father. He would never forget it. Maria, from that moment on, became very quiet, and only rarely would speak at all. They both held each other and tried to live on, but it wasn't easy.

1

SIXTEEN YEARS LATER
MAY 28, 1684

As Diego left his house, just a short way from the bay where construction was going on for the new fortress that the Governor was trying to complete, he looked over to see that, once again, no one was working on it.

He had been just a boy of six when those terrible pirates came and attacked the village, but his mother rushed him, and several other children, from the cottage into the nearby woods to hide. Many other people also disappeared into the woods. But many of those who stayed to protect their homes did not survive, including his father.

That was sixteen years ago, and he still remembered it like it was yesterday.

Just four years later, there was much excitement about the Spanish Crown building a stone fortress to replace the old, dilapidated wooden one.

The townspeople were happy, but although it was a good start, over the next few years, many things slowed the construction, sometimes to a stop.

There had been several changes in Governors, and as one died off, and another arrived and took over the promised financing from Spain became unreliable and often slow in coming. Thus, the men working on the construction would leave for other means of income.

Diego thought to himself, *'will anyone ever make life here safe and secure?'* Anyway, he had to feed his new family. So, to the shore and the boats, he went.

He had married Luisa just a year ago and, although still living in the cottage with his mother, the three of them needed to eat; and their small garden couldn't provide enough for them. He recently found that Luisa was pregnant, which was going to be another burden on his shoulders.

He got to his boat and saw that he was earlier than all the other fishermen, and he pushed off and began to row out into the bay. It was that time of year that the often-desired Redfish were running, and he would try to catch enough of them today so that he would be able to trade them for some cotton cloth and wool for the family and still put dinner on the table.

After about seven hours, Diego tied his boat to the shore and carried a basket of fifteen good-sized Redfish towards the village's center. It wasn't a lot, but probably enough to get the wool and cloth his wife and mother needed.

As he walked by, he looked over at the Castillo construction site and noticed that, as if by magic, men were again working on the structure. He resolved to see if he could join their ranks tomorrow, and maybe earn a better living.

When he got to the center and stepped into the store of Señor Riguez, he hoped that these large Redfish, he had caught, would be enough to trade for the needed materials. It was close, but Señor Riguez had been a friend of Diego's father, those many years ago, and knew that this young man was trying very hard to keep his family together.

He said to Diego: "I'll take thirteen of those fish for the wool, and I have some five '*vara*' (yards) of cotton cloth that was returned unused; I give you that as well. Together they are worth about one 'Peso' and five 'Reales,' a fair exchange for thirteen Redfish."

Diego was happy to still have two sizeable Redfish for their dinner tonight, and the materials would please both Luisa and his mother. So, after thanking Señor Riguez, he took the wool and cloth and headed home.

The next morning, Diego went to the government house to see if there was any work that he could do at the new fortress. If so, he could earn some much-needed Pesos.

His timing was right, for the need for more coquina blocks was going to be the next big challenge for the builders.

The added fact that he owned a flatboat that could tow the massive blocks, loaded on rafts, was a decisive point in his favor. That, and there was a need for all additional labor available at the time.

The wage he could earn was seven Pesos a month and would be enough for Luisa and his family to be more comfortable and help prepare for the birth of their child.

After reporting to the head builder at the site, he was given a parchment slip, with a Royal Seal, that stated he was now a government employee. He was then told to report to the quarry, across the bay, over on Anastasia Island.

When Diego got over there, he was surprised to see at least a dozen other men working in the ever-increasing quarry. They were using hammers and picks to split off the large pieces of the coquina, many of which had to weigh five hundred libras (pounds) or more.

As he reported for work, the quarry master saw that he had a boat, and assigned him to begin the transport of many of the massive blocks lined along the shore.

With the help of several other men, including several from the local nearby Timucua tribe, they began loading the mostly dried blocks onto the rafts. Then, one-at-a-time, he began to tow them across the bay to the shore by the new construction site. Although there were men available to help unload the coquina, it was blistering hard work.

After three hard days of work, Diego was glad to rest on that Sunday; when Luisa and his mother got ready early and they all walked past the silent construction site to the small chapel of Our Lady of La Leche for the redemption message the priest would give.

Luisa had harvested several select vegetables from their garden and packaged them carefully to give as an offering to the mission. It was a simple gesture, but one they would always honor.

Diego was happy to spend the day with his family and found that he began to relax and would even help his mother and Luisa with a few chores around their small house.

However, Monday morning came soon, and he was back at work, towing the massive coquina blocks across the bay.

The day went by quickly, as Diego made trip after trip across the bay; first towing the massive blocks of coquina then, almost as if to reward his effort, he simply pulled the empty rafts back to Anastasia Island. To be loaded again.

He had placed his fishing equipment in the boat, and when there was a break for lunch, or when the next raft wasn't ready to tow yet, he would cast his hook into the bay, hoping to catch something for dinner. He had told Luisa to come down to the shore early each afternoon and see if he had a green piece of cloth hanging on a stick on the front of his boat. If she saw it, she would wait on the shore, take the basket with the dinner fish in it, and head back home.

For the most part, their system worked well; the family would have fresh fish for dinner or be able to trade for some chicken or lamb, and yet spend none of the hard-earned wages to purchase it.

The work did tire Diego, and at sundown, as he would head home, he would look forward to a warm dinner and a good night's sleep. Of course, he did need to spend some time with both Luisa and his ailing mother. He had noticed a week ago that his mother was having a hard time breathing and needed to stay warm sitting by the cooking fire much of the day.

On Wednesday, soon after he left for work, his mother's breathing simply stopped. She was gone.

Luisa stood at the shore, waiting for him to tow the massive raft across the bay to tell him of her passing.

As Diego bowed his head and crossed himself, his mind went back to the days after his father, and so many other townspeople died. Lessons learned from that time taught him that it was necessary to get the body beneath the ground as soon as possible. He needed, however, the approval and blessings from a priest.

Taking Luisa's hand, they walked together to the small chapel at Our Lady of La Leche to find the Friar and ask for his advice and instructions.

It was too late in the day to have the burial, so they had to wait for the next morning.

Right to the Friar's word, a little after first light the next morning, four men from town accompanied the Friar to Diego's house. They placed the body in a simple pine box and carried it off to the cemetery.

After the Friar's Prayers, Diego and the four men put the coffin in the ground and began to cover it with the earth.

Luisa, saddened by Diego's loss, stayed by his side until they finally left for home. She had realized that it was now she who must have control of the household, and there was no one else to turn to for guidance.

With that thought still in her mind, a kick in her belly reminded her that soon there would be another responsibility they both needed to face.

The next morning, Diego was back to work, again towing coquina blocks across the bay.

The work on Castillo was moving along, and Diego felt a little proud of himself for being a part, albeit only a small part, of the project that would help protect their community.

As he went to the shore, each day, he would look over at the soldados who were manning the wooden fort just south of the new construction site. They always seemed to be watching the workmen at the fort and occasionally practicing with cannon shots over the bay.

Diego knew most of these men, for they were his neighbors in the town. They spent just three days a week at the stockade, then most of them also worked on various parts of the construction project when their duty times were over.

There was a need for the city economy to prosper, and, in somewhat unorthodox ways, it did. Not all transactions involved actual money; much of it was a trade of products and services. The values of specific items became established over time, and the tradesmen knew what those were.

There was cash, of course, and its value was undisputed. Still, the continuing unreliable and unpredictable funding from the Spanish Crown made the daily use of the item for item trading a reliable backup.

Diego, as he realized that he needed to keep his growing family cared for, started to do more fishing each day as he rowed back and forth across the bay. He had found he could usually catch three or four fish on most days.

Occasionally, there was a day when the weather was not favorable for towing coquina, and he would spend that time hunting in the nearby woods with the matchlock musket that had been his father's many years ago.

An occasional deer or a wild boar was a treat for both he and Luisa.

In the evening, while sitting by the cooking fire, Diego is worried and concerned about his family and their future.

His thoughts would go to what tomorrow would bring, more uncertainty, more struggles, or less? What will lie past this moment, just dreams, maybe hopes?

With the death of his mother still in his mind, he looked over at Luisa and thought about their child's future birth. It brings him to a sobering moment; he will soon be a father. It is something he never really considered before. From the age of six, he never knew what a father's guidance could mean to a child.

Diego holds onto his faith, thankful for God's strength to toil, albeit with a constant struggle and willingness to push through in the hopes of "just maybe."

His thoughts drift to the present, and he begins to question what was happening around him. *'Was the Castillo being built for the love of King and country? Was it for España? Was it for the Colony's betterment and the protection of the people, his people, his family, himself? Who is our enemy? What makes them our enemy?'*

Those thoughts kept forming in his head, and as he closed his eyes and prepared for the next day's work, he began to wonder how long this project would take and what was in the future when it was complete.

Perhaps those thoughts were a forbearing of what was to come, for Diego found, later that next week, that the construction funds had, again, run out.

King Charles II, in España, had wasted much. Still, it was his mother, Queen Regent Mariana, who, when he was a child, initially provided funding for the Castillo and, although getting old, still had some influence over the King.

The acknowledgment that funds were no longer currently available came from the building supervisors. They told of delays in funding from España, hoping that it would return again soon.

Something in the way they spoke led Diego to begin and wonder what he should do. No, what he must do. His home, his wife, their future child, his community all must come first.

He knew that some of the workers would continue with the Castillo, and he would help with it as best he could. But the other things had to be done first.

He began to work only half a day, towing the coquina across the bay and spending the rest of the day fishing for the support of his family. Most of the other men who had been working on the Castillo left for any additional work they could find. Some, like Diego, continued to do some work with the hope the funds would soon return.

Many men needed to find another way to survive, so the construction work continued to slow again as they kept leaving.

Many of them needed to continue their lives and moved away from Saint Augustine, sometimes signing aboard ships that would take them down to the more developed areas in the Caribbean.

The government officials tried to keep things going, but as before, without reliable funding, the community began to shrink and become more impoverished.

Diego was, at least, a fisherman; and was able to catch enough to trade for the much-needed items for his family. But it had become a slim existence again. Even the Sunday trips to church, had Luisa taking smaller vegetable offerings with them.

$$\bullet\;3\;\bullet$$

Diego thought back to when both Luisa and he had spent much of their teenage childhood years in the local Friar's daily care.

Luisa, as an only child, and two years younger than Diego and had lost both her father and mother when their home collapsed in a hurricane eight years ago. At the age of twelve, she was taken in by her mother's elderly aunt and uncle.

Although they cared and provided for her, they were not her parents, and they never had children themselves. So, they decided that the church's influence would be best for her day-to-day life.

Friar Jose Sanchez of the small chapel at Our Lady of La Leche was a kind man, and he realized that there were things she could do by helping with much of the chapel's daily care.

It was about that same time that Diego, also a bit of a lost soul, at fourteen years of age, came to the Friar looking for some work he could do to help his mother. Maria had worked at sewing and weaving blankets and clothing to provide for their existence, but it left little time for Diego.

The Friar gave each of them things to do that would lessen their burden, and at the same time, help the church; but he also thought they would be better Catholics if he taught them to read and write. So, he resolved to give each of them lessons three times a week.

During the in-between times, Luisa was put to work dusting and cleaning the chapel, and Diego was assigned to apprentice for one of the local men with instructions to care for the church's flatboat and learn to fish.

As time went by, failing health changes found that Luisa was needed to aid and help care for the aging Friar. Although helping out at the chapel when he could, Diego was now working as a full-time fisherman, with his own flatboat that he had built, to provide for himself and his mother.

He would, however, spend almost all of his free time at the mission, assuring that the care of their flatboat was maintained and that there was fresh fish available. Also, he liked to be around Luisa whenever he could, and they would sit together and read many of the notes and books that Friar Sanchez had left for them.

Both Luisa and Diego found that there was more reward to their being together, while in the church's care than they had first thought, and they would usually spend most of their free time with each other.

About a year and a half ago, Diego went to see both the aging Friar Sanchez and Luisa's great uncle and was granted permission to marry her.

Diego's mother, Maria, was happy to see Diego and Luisa together, and they, all three, worked together to expand the cottage to accommodate each of them.

It was the first time in Luisa's adult life that she had a woman to help guide her in the household duties of a wife. After years of struggling to be a mother and provider at the same time, Maria was glad to have Luisa there and became quite fond of her as well.

As the first year of their life together passed, Diego was becoming more and more capable of providing for his new expanded family. However, with the unreliable funding of the Castillo and the reduction in income, he needed to spend more time as a commercial fisherman.

He was able to catch enough fish for most days to trade for needed goods and even to sell to several local shops.

It had become evident to Diego that he must improve the situation he was in, assuring his family's safety. Several of his neighbors found themselves in a similar situation.

It was becoming a frequent point of discussion amongst the men in his neighborhood. Those points were exacerbated by the social differences that were common in Saint Augustine and throughout the Spanish colonies.

Diego, like many of his neighbors, were ‹Criollos› (people mostly of Spanish or European heritage, born in the new world) and although legally Spaniards, they were socially ranked below the government officials and those of the upper-class controlling authority, who were mostly ‹Peninsulares› (people born in Spain of Spanish parents).

Many of the lower classes of people, 'Mulattos' (people of mixed race) had an even harder time earning a decent living, but together they were all part of the community. It was, however, the Catholic church that had the common ground, and it did much to hold things together. Also, there was always allegiance to the King.

Diego and the other men would talk about the future, hoping that the construction would again become the primary source of income for their community.

$$4$$

Diego was just eighteen years old when Governor Pablo_de_Hita_y_Salazar was recalled to for making alterations to Castillo's construction plans and replaced by Governor Juan Márquez Cabrera.

Governor Cabrera was known to be a bit abusive to the general population, and many of those like Diego were happy to avoid his attention whenever possible. He did, however, maintain control, and there was a feeling of security under his command.

With the passage of time and recent happenings, Diego was becoming more concerned; and with the birth of their child coming soon, he realized that he must be prepared to provide for his family and protect them as well.

Security had become more the point of discussion amongst the men in town, and they all had found a need to understand just who was their potential enemy, and why?

Discussions of the British having occupied and now expanding a coastal town only two sailing days away, in that area known as 'Charles Town' in the southern part of the Carolinas, was one of the main deciding reasons for the construction of the stone Castillo.

The townspeople knew that the British had been fighting the Spanish Crown for years, and now that fight was continuing to come closer to here, in New Spain. Although they didn't all understand what the argument was about, they all knew their very lives and those of their families were in danger if the British ever came.

They also knew the Spanish fleets used their port as the last supply stop on their way back to Spain, and that the town's existence and economy depended upon much of the resulting trade.

Together, these men, neighbors, and friends were becoming more and more concerned and even afraid. Many found strength in joining the Soldado's and the Spanish army. In contrast, many others swore allegiance to the King and, although originally created for those of low social status, joined with the local militia.

It was there that Diego found his place. He could continue to find supplies and provide for his family yet be a member ready and able to defend his home and town.

A week later, with the arrival of three Spanish ships, word quickly went out that additional funds had been promised, and work on the Castillo could again resume.

It was a slow return, as work on the Castillo started up again. Many of the skilled workers had found other sources of income, and others had left Saint Augustine for work in faraway places. But the work did continue, and with the help of local native Timucua, Guale, and Apalachee Indians, progress was beginning to show.

The outside dimensions of the structure were complete, and the thick walls were getting higher. For the most part, the wall had reached almost its intended finished height of twenty-seven '*Pie*' (feet) along the eastern shoreline. The cannon bastions, located at each of the four corners, would be the most substantial part and used up a large amount of coquina.

Although it was slow to progress, skilled workers did begin to return from Cuba and other Caribbean islands. Even some Cuban convicts were brought along with them to provide additional Labor. Diego returned to the full-time work of towing coquina across the bay, but he had learned that fishing was still a needed addition to his efforts.

Diego wanted to keep his obligation to the construction of the Castillo, yet also assure Luisa that he was always going to be there for her and their future child. That meant that earning a reliable income was still the primary challenge.

So, he would spend as much time as he could fishing and towing coquina; yet look to other tasks he could do to assure their safety. He found that his skill at the construction of flatboats was needed, and several people were looking for the repair or replacement of them.

So, his workweek became even longer as he tried to get as much done as he could. However, Sunday was the Lord's day of rest. Both he and Luisa would spend much of it at the mission, but always together.

Ironically, Friar Sanchez's eyesight had been failing, and it left him with the inability to read the gospel and the passages he loved so much. So, on those Sunday's when Diego and Luisa could spend time with the Friar, they would take turns reading the passages aloud to him as he sat quietly and listened with his eyes closed.

～❦ 5 ❦～

The summer months passed slowly, and Luisa became more uncomfortable as the baby's birth was getting near. The summer months were frequently hot, and when there was little or no breeze, it was challenging to even move about in their house. She found it often necessary to keep a wet towel or bonnet on her head to stay cool, and her movements slowed down.

Diego was concerned for her and did his best to try and help out whenever he could. But this was something neither of them knew anything about or had any experience.

Luisa found that when she could walk to the town, she would usually feel a little better and could get needed items for the care of their house. On several trips to town, she stopped in at the store owned by Señor Riguez.

Late in August, she stopped in to see if she could buy a few 'vara' of cotton cloth that when wet, she could hang in the windows of the house, and the breeze would somehow cool the home to a more comfortable condition.

Although she knew Señor Riguez, this day, he was busy in the back of his store, and an older woman came over to help her find what was needed. It was his wife who just happened to be there that day. Señora Elana Riguez could not help but see that Luisa was pregnant and getting very near her time, so she made Luisa sit down and did the necessary shopping for her.

Elana Riguez had known Maria Rivera and knew that her son Diego was married to Luisa. But she hadn't realized that she was pregnant. She asked Luisa who was available to help her through the birth of her child and was surprised to learn that Luisa, with her head bowed, said there was no one to help her other than Diego.

Elana decided at that moment that she would become the midwife for Luisa when the child was born. She instructed her to tell Diego that he was to come to get her and that she would be there from the moment her Labor began. With mixed emotions, Luisa was thankful for Señora Riguez's attention and yet felt guilty, realizing that there was a need for it.

Diego could see that Luisa was trying to keep up with the house and the chores of cooking and cleaning but was becoming unable to hide her discomfort. He found that his caring for Luisa was an even stronger feeling than he thought and knew he must become more of a help around the house.

The timing for their child's birth was suddenly upon them when Luisa let out a scream of agony late in the evening on the first Monday of September.

Luisa had followed Señora Riguez's instructions to tell Diego, and he went right away and got her. It was a rough night, and it wasn't till almost noon of the following day that their child was born.

Diego was instructed to remain out of the room while Luisa was in Labor, and, although he didn't want to, he followed their wishes even when he heard Luisa scream or when the new baby cried. It was a relief to him when Señora Riguez came out of the room with the baby, wrapped in a towel, in her arms. She told him Luisa was alright and that she was now resting.

With that, she handed the baby carefully to Diego and said, with a smile: "Meet your new daughter Diego."

Diego took the infant and held her carefully as he stared at her. A daughter! He and Luisa hadn't thought much about the sex of their child, but he had just assumed it would be a boy. Now a flood of emotions swept over him as he realized that he was the father of a little girl.

Without asking, he carried his daughter into the room where Luisa was resting, smiled down at her and said: "She is beautiful, what shall we name her?"

He was surprised when she said to him: "Your mother knew we were going to have a baby, but she did not get to see her, can we name her Maria after your mother?"

Diego was silent for several moments and looking down at her then over to Señora Riguez said: "We have been through much together, Luisa, and when help was needed, somehow it always found us. I believe we need to be thankful for those who were always there. So, will you agree that her name shall be Maria Elana?"

As a new life began for the Rivera family of Diego, Luisa, and Maria Elana, the workload on Diego was again going to be a little harder, but he did not worry about that. Luisa, too, had much more to do now, and although she was back to being herself again, the added care needed for Maria Elana was a drain on her.

Diego was back towing coquina two days later and was grateful that Señora Riguez would stop by almost every day to check on Luisa and Maria Elana. The value of the small town and the neighbors who lived there became more relevant to them every day.

EPILOGUE

By the end of the year of 1684, life for Diego, Luisa, and Maria Elana had settled into a day-to-day routine; that was what the average Spanish citizen of Saint Augustine had come to experience.

It had been a pivotal year for both of them. Together Diego and Luisa had seen life changes that included the death of Diego's mother and continuing on and off construction on the Castillo, after some time of slow funding.

Diego continued to use his abilities in aid to that construction whenever he could. He had improved his ability to feed and reliably care for his family, and still be prepared to defend them.

Luisa had also learned much that year. Like Diego, she had grown up without the typical guidance that her parents would provide. The church had taught her many helpful things, but it was only after she and Diego were married that she had his mother to help guide her in the typical household duties.

With the birth of Maria Elana, they both realized that they were now the ones to provide the necessary guidance. They learned that neighbors were often available when needed, and they resolved to give back to their community whenever possible.

Two years after the birth of Maria Elana, Luisa gave birth to a second child, a son named Jose Pedro, named after the Friar and Diego's father. It turned out that two-year-old Maria Elana was a good big sister to her little brother. Diego was happy to have a boy who would someday be able to work with him.

Lessons they learned from Friar Sanchez as they grew up followed them throughout their lives. The church was always a very important thing, and their faith in God would never leave them.

It was very unusual that both Luisa and Diego could read and write, for it was rare for anyone not born of the aristocracy to have that skill. It was almost unheard of for a woman, and even then, it was only rarely found in the church.

But as Maria Elana and Jose Pedro grew older, Luisa decided that she would not only pass on that skill to them but began to hold classes for several other young children from town as well.

As the next ten years passed, the city of Saint Augustine continued to grow. There were still times when things slowed nearly to a stop, but, somehow, it continued to prosper. By the end of 1695, the Castillo was complete, and the old, dilapidated wooden fortress was gone.

Diego continued fishing and also became a fine carpenter who could build flatboats for some of the other men in the town. As Jose Pedro grew older, he would help his father build the boats, but his real interest was in the care of horses and cattle.

At the age of ten, Jose Pedro became a stable lad in the town's central stable and was given the task of caring for Governor Laureano_de_Torres_y_Ayala.

Three years later, when the Governor changed again, Jose Pedro, an excellent horseman, became a young drover for several cattle ranches in the surrounding area and would bring herds to Saint Augustine for slaughter.

Maria Elana also grew to be a valuable citizen of her town. Much to the pride of her father and mother, she became an aid to the health of her neighbors and an experienced midwife by the age of seventeen.

Life for Diego and Luisa was more secure as time went by, and they both found peace in the knowledge that their children were prepared for the future.

But the never-ending threat of invasion from the British, pirates, or even others, was always there. It proved to be true when, seven years after the completion of the Castillo de San Marcos, the British did attack; and in force to take and occupy the city not long before Christmas time.

It was with renewed fear that Diego and Luisa, along with Maria Elana and Jose Pedro, went with almost fifteen hundred other town people into the Castillo, where they would remain for fifty-one days.

Diego and Jose Pedro joined with the soldados on the gun deck in the fight, while Luisa and Maria Elana worked tirelessly, helping care for those who needed help.

It was a new generation of people that were now going to have the responsibility of protecting their homes, and both eighteen-year-old Maria Elana and sixteen-year-old Jose Pedro were ready to join in and pick up the task.

When the siege was raised, after nearly two months, the family returned to their burned down-home. It was with tears in their eyes but resolve in their hearts that they began to rebuild again.

LA HISTORIA DE DIEGO EN SAN AGUSTIN 1684

Las siguientes páginas representan una historia ficticia que describe el día a día de una pequeña familia que vive en la segunda mitad del siglo XVII en la ciudad de San Agustín, Florida.

Aunque las referencias a de los eventos históricos específicos son reales, los nombres, las acciones y declaraciones de los personajes son de la imaginación del autor y no representan hechos reales.

Hay áreas donde la información histórica ha venido de fuentes desconocidas o múltiples fuentes no identificadas.

Con esto en mente, todas las contribuciones de fuentes conocidas y desconocidas son muy apreciadas y reconocidas.

Es con apreciación adicional que el conocimiento del período de tiempo mencionado se proporciona a través de los esfuerzos de muchos recreadores voluntarios que, junto con el autor, intentan dar vida, a la historia de los españoles y sus familias, para los muchos visitantes que vienen a la ciudad continuamente ocupada más antigua de América, San Agustín, Florida.

PRÓLOGO
28 DE MAYO DE 1668

Pedro Rivera no podía dormir. Por alguna razón, se había despertado y luego se levantó de la cama para escuchar de nuevo el sonido que creía haber percibido. Estaba muy oscuro afuera, y todavía unas cuatro horas antes de la primera luz del día, pero había luz de luna, y el resplandor era suficiente para que se moviera en su pequeña cabaña sin despertar a su esposa María o a su hijo Diego.

Comenzó a pensar que lo había imaginado, cuando volvió a escuchar, a lo lejos, varios disparos de mosquete y alguien gritando. Estaba demasiado lejos para que escuchara lo que se decía, pero había un tono de miedo que despertaba alarma.

Durante ciento tres años, el pequeño y remoto pueblo de San Agustín, en el extremo norte de la Florida española, había pasado de ser un pequeño puesto militar a una pequeña ciudad próspera. Aunque lejos de las ciudades caribeñas controladas por los españoles, estaban en una buena posición, lo suficientemente cerca de la frontera norte, para evitar una posible intervención británica en el territorio español reclamado de La Florida.

Aunque su economía estaba creciendo, muchas de las necesidades cotidianas de la ciudad todavía eran abastecidas por los barcos españoles que navegarían hacia el norte a lo largo de la costa oriental de la península de La Florida. Los suministros de alimentos de harina, granos y varios otros artículos necesarios para esta remota ciudad ocasionalmente se enviaban desde Veracruz, México y varias islas del Caribe controladas por los españoles.

Aunque generalmente se solicitaban envíos de estos y otros artículos diversos, las comunicaciones fiables entre San Agustín y las grandes ciudades del Caribe en el mejor de los casos era esporádico y en el peor inexistente. Sin embargo, actualmente se debía entregar un cargamento de granos y harina muy necesarios; Pero se había retrasado varios días con respecto a su llegada programada.

Las condiciones climáticas eran buenas, por lo que, con preocupación, el Presidio de San Agustín había enviado su propia fragata con instrucciones de navegar hacia el sur y tratar de encontrar el barco atrasado y su carga.

A última hora de la tarde del 28 de mayo de 1668, dos barcos en dirección norte fueron avistados frente a la costa sur. Pronto se hizo evidente que esos barcos eran, de hecho, los buques esperados, ya que uno de ellos era su propia fragata; Pero llegarían demasiado tarde para desembarcar hoy. Por lo tanto, anclarían en alta mar y esperarían hasta la mañana.

Fue con alivio que Don Francisco de la Guerra y de la Vega, el gobernador de La Florida ordenó a los soldados de la guarnición que colocaran sus mosquetes de cerilla en la caseta de guardia, a un cuarto de milla del fuerte en la ciudad, y se fueran a casa a dormir.

Como lo hizo muchas noches, el cabo Miguel de Monzón había salido de su casa tarde esa noche y se había ido a pescar, en su canoa.

Alrededor de la 1:00 a.m., escuchó el sonido de muchos remos tirando sobre el agua, y en la oscuridad, rápidamente se dio cuenta de que no era bueno que tantos botes largos estuvieran en la orilla a esa hora y se movió para hacer sonar la alarma. Cuando comenzó a remar hacia el muelle de la ciudad, los corsarios corrieron tras él y le dispararon dos veces cuando llegó a la orilla.

Aunque herido, Monzón comenzó a gritar una advertencia tardía y logró llegar a la seguridad de la fortaleza de madera en descomposición de la ciudad. Detrás de él, los bucaneros irrumpieron en tierra.

Probablemente fueron esos disparos de mosquete y los gritos del Cabo Monzón los que despertaron a Pedro, y ahora podía escuchar gritos y ruidos adicionales.

La gente del pueblo fue tomada completamente por sorpresa cuando grupos de piratas corrieron por las calles, gritando y con frecuencia capturando o disparando a los habitantes asustados y somnolientos cuando salían de sus hogares.

Cuando los funcionarios del gobierno también escucharon el ruido y se dieron cuenta de lo que estaba sucediendo, el oficial superior de la guarnición del presidio, el sargento mayor Nicolás Ponce de León, corrió rápidamente a la caseta de vigilancia solo para descubrir que ya había sido capturada y saqueada.

Mientras los grupos de piratas se formaban en el fuerte listos para precipitarse hacia él, el Sargento Mayor pudo reunir y guiar a más de cien hombres desconcertados, mujeres, niños e incluso algunos soldados desarmados, a un lugar seguro en el bosque a una legua de distancia.

Pedro, después de escuchar los gritos desde dos calles de distancia, entonces, al escuchar los disparos de mosquetes, se dio cuenta de que la ciudad estaba bajo ataque. Desde la cama en la habitación de la esquina de su pequeña cabaña, escuchó a su esposa María decir: "Pedro, ¿qué está pasando?"

Él respondió: «Vístete para el bosque, viaja rápidamente, y asegúrate de que Diego también esté vestido para el bosque; la ciudad está siendo atacada».

Mientras María llamaba a Diego y luchaban por vestirse, Pedro agarró su mosquete de cerilla y, mientras deslizaba el cinturón de pólvora de los "doce apóstoles" sobre su hombro, se volvió hacia la puerta y escuchó gritos de varios de sus vecinos que también se preparaban para correr y esconderse.

Fue entonces cuando escuchó al sargento mayor Nicolás Ponce de León gritar a los residentes cercanos que siguieran su ejemplo hacia el bosque y la seguridad.

Dirigiéndose a María y a su hijo Diego, de seis años, dijo: "Ve, María, sigue al 'Sargento Mayor' al bosque, me quedaré y ayudaré a defender nuestro hogar".

María, conociendo a su esposo, no pudo decir nada que cambiara su opinión; entonces, ella lo abrazó una vez más, tomó a Diego de la mano y huyó por la puerta para escapar con tantas otras mujeres y niños.

Pedro se puso de pie y los vio desaparecer en los pinos y palmeras que rodeaban su casa hasta que ya no pudo verlos. Se volvió hacia el crucifijo en la pared, cayó de rodillas y oró para que ellos y su ciudad sobrevivieran.

Un golpe en la puerta reveló a siete de sus vecinos, todos vestidos como él con armas y pólvora listos para defender su ciudad. Rápidamente se unió a sus filas, y se extendieron alrededor de cualquier barrera defensiva que pudieron encontrar y apuntaron a los piratas mientras corrían por la calle.

Otros asaltantes cruzaron la plaza de la ciudad y entraron en la Casa de Gobierno, el gobernador Francisco de la Guerra y de la Vega los había visto acercarse y sabía que tenía que salir y dirigirse al fuerte. Debe defenderlo, ya que era uno de sus principales deberes como gobernador.

Una puerta oculta fue su escape, y, con los piratas siguiéndole los talones, llegó al recinto del fuerte junto con varios otros refugiados. Los que estaban en el fuerte ya estaban alertados por el ruido del fuego de mosquete, ~~gritos~~ y gritos de miedo.

Cuando se le notificó de la incursión, el oficial de turno del fuerte, el capitán Mateo Pacheco Salgado, alertó a las tropas de servicio. Abrieron la puerta del recinto para admitir al gobernador y otros funcionarios reales, y un puñado de hombres adicionales. El gobernador inmediatamente tomó el mando de los treinta y tres hombres disponibles.

La empalizada era vieja y ruinosa, con paredes y cubiertas de madera, pero les daba el terreno elevado para la defensa. El gobernador ordenó inmediatamente abrir el polvorín y distribuyó municiones a los soldados que estaban presentes, pero antes de que los cañones pudieran cargarse, los piratas atacaron la fortaleza.

Los corsarios intentaron repetidamente asaltar las paredes durante la siguiente hora y media, solo para ser rechazados por el intenso fuego de mosquete.

Los bucaneros finalmente se retiraron, con once de sus hombres muertos y diecinueve heridos.

Más al sur, en la ciudad, la milicia ciudadana que incluía a Pedro Rivera se vio abrumada por la gran cantidad de piratas y su despiadado deseo de saquear todas las casas y edificios.

Cuando dos de esos bandidos vinieron corriendo hacia los hombres, Pedro y su vecino Carlos, ambos dispararon al mismo tiempo y los vieron caer, mientras las balas de mosquete golpeaban a ambos en el medio de sus pechos.

Ambos hombres se pusieron de pie para recargar, y luego, al mismo tiempo, ellos también fueron alcanzados por fuego de mosquete, pero esta vez fue de piratas que cargaban desde el otro lado. La muerte fue rápida, y tanto Pedro como Carlos cayeron al suelo encima de sus mosquetes.

Nunca lo sabrían, pero con la luz del día llegó otro barco. Era el propio barco del capitán pirata Robert Searle, el 'Cagway' de sesenta toneladas. Llegó y ancló en la bahía junto a los otros dos buques.

El barco Veracruz había sido capturada en alta mar unos días antes, y cuando apareció la fragata del Presidio, también fue capturada cuando encontró al Veracruz. Ambos barcos fueron dirigidos a San Agustín por los piratas, y ahora estaban anclados en la bahía.

Después del ataque nocturno en la orilla, los corsarios regresaron para completar el saqueo de San Agustín a la luz del día. Incluso la iglesia parroquial y las capillas de los conventos franciscanos no fueron perdonadas y ellos también perderían todos sus ornamentos.

Las casas fueron registradas y robadas de todos los objetos de valor. El botín fue transportado y cargado a bordo del Cagway y el barco desde Veracruz.

Pasarían varios días antes de que aquellos que habían sobrevivido en el bosque pudieran regresar a la carnicería que había sido su hogar. Todavía había muchos cadáveres tirados en la calle, y el olor era espantoso.

Junto con muchos de sus vecinos, María y Diego regresaron a la devastación y comenzaron la tarea de encontrar a sus familiares muertos y ver por los entierros lo mejor que pudieron.

Diego, de seis años, creció diez años en su mente, si no en su cuerpo, cuando vio a su padre. Nunca lo olvidaría. María, a partir de ese momento, se volvió muy callada, y rara vez hablaba. Ambos se abrazaron y trataron de seguir viviendo, pero no fue fácil.

1

DIECISÉIS AÑOS DESPUÉS
28 DE MAYO DE 1684

Cuando Diego salió de su casa, a poca distancia de la bahía donde se estaba construyendo la nueva fortaleza que el Gobernador estaba tratando de completar, miró para ver que, una vez más, nadie estaba trabajando en ella.

Era solo un niño de seis años cuando esos terribles piratas llegaron y atacaron el pueblo, pero su madre lo apresuró a él, y a varios otros niños, de la cabaña a los bosques cercanos para esconderse. Muchas otras personas también desaparecieron en el bosque. Pero muchos de los que se quedaron para proteger sus hogares no sobrevivieron, incluido su padre.

Eso fue hace dieciséis años, y todavía lo recordaba como si fuera ayer.

Solo cuatro años después, hubo mucha emoción por la construcción de la Corona española de una fortaleza de piedra para reemplazar la vieja y derruida de madera.

La gente del pueblo estaba contenta, pero, aunque fue un buen comienzo, en los próximos años, muchas cosas ralentizaron la construcción, a veces hasta detenerse.

Hubo varios cambios de gobernadores, y cuando uno murió, y otro llegó y se hizo cargo de la financiación prometida de España, esta se volvió poco confiable y a menudo tardó en llegar. Por lo tanto, los hombres que trabajaban en la construcción se irían a acogerían otros medios de ingresos.

Diego pensó para sí mismo, *"¿Alguien alguna vez hará que la vida aquí sea segura y protegida?* "De todos modos, tenía que alimentar a su nueva familia. Así que, a la orilla y a los barcos, se fue.

Se había casado con Luisa hacía apenas un año y, aunque todavía vivía en la cabaña con su madre, los tres necesitaban comer; y su pequeño jardín no podía proporcionarles lo suficiente. Recientemente descubrió que Luisa estaba embarazada, lo que iba a ser otra carga sobre sus hombros.

Llegó a su bote y vio que estaba antes que todos los demás pescadores, por lo que comenzó a remar hacia la bahía. Era esa época del año en que la gallineta nórdica a menudo deseada se encontraba cerca de la bahía, y él trataría de atrapar suficientes de ellas para poder cambiarlas por un poco de tela de algodón y lana para la familia y poner la cena en la mesa.

Después de unas siete horas, Diego ató su bote a la orilla y llevó una canasta de quince gallinetas nórdicas de buen tamaño hacia el centro del pueblo. No era mucho, pero probablemente lo suficiente para conseguir la lana y la tela que su esposa y su madre necesitaban.

Mientras pasaba, miró hacia el sitio de construcción de Castillo y notó que, como por arte de magia, los hombres estaban trabajando nuevamente en la estructura. Decidió ver si podía unirse a sus filas mañana, y tal vez ganarse la vida mejor.

Cuando llegó al centro y entró en la tienda del Señor Ríguez, esperaba que estas grandes gallinetas, que había capturado, fueran suficientes para intercambiar los materiales necesarios. Estaba cerca, pero el Señor Riguez había sido amigo del padre de Diego, desde ~~hace~~ hacía muchos años, y sabía que este joven estaba tratando muy duro de mantener unida a su familia.

Le dijo a Diego: "Tomaré trece de esos peces para la lana, y tengo unas cinco varas (*yards*) de tela de algodón que se devolvieron sin usar; Te doy eso también. Juntos valen alrededor de un 'peso' y cinco 'reales', un intercambio justo por trece gallinetas".

Diego estaba feliz de tener dos gallinetas nórdicas para su cena de esa noche, y los materiales complacerían tanto a Luisa como a su madre. Entonces, después de agradecer al Señor Riguez, tomó la lana y la tela y se dirigió a casa.

A la mañana siguiente, Diego fue a la casa de gobierno para ver si había algún trabajo que pudiera hacer en la nueva fortaleza. Si es así, podría ganar algunos pesos muy necesarios.

Su momento era el correcto, ya que la necesidad de más bloques de coquina iba a ser el próximo gran desafío para los constructores.

El hecho adicional de que poseía un bote plano que podía remolcar los bloques masivos, cargados en balsas, fue un punto decisivo a su favor. Eso, y había una necesidad de toda la mano de obra adicional disponible en ese momento.

El salario que podía ganar era de siete pesos al mes y sería suficiente para que Luisa y su familia estuvieran más cómodos y ayudaran a prepararse para el nacimiento de su hijo.

Después de informar al jefe de obras en el sitio, se le dio un recibo de pergamino, con un sello real, que decía que ahora era un empleado del gobierno. Luego le dijeron que se presentara en la cantera, al otro lado de la bahía, en la isla Anastasia.

Cuando Diego llegó allí, se sorprendió al ver al menos a una docena de otros hombres trabajando en la cantera cada vez mayor. Usaban martillos y picos para separar los grandes trozos de la coquina, muchos de los cuales tenían que pesar quinientas libras o más.

Mientras se preparaba para comenzar a trabajar, el maestro de la cantera vio que tenía un bote y le asignó comenzar el transporte de muchos de los bloques masivos alineados a lo largo de la orilla.

Con la ayuda de varios otros hombres, incluidos varios de la tribu local cercana Timucua, comenzaron a cargar los bloques en su mayoría secos en las balsas. Luego, uno a la vez, comenzó a remolcarlos a través de la bahía hasta la orilla del nuevo sitio de construcción. Aunque había hombres disponibles para ayudar a descargar la coquina, era un trabajo muy duro.

Después de tres fatigosos y arduos días de trabajo, Diego se alegró de descansar ese domingo; cuando Luisa y su madre se prepararon temprano y todos pasaron por el sitio de construcción silencioso en esos momentos hasta la pequeña capilla de Nuestra Señora de La Leche para el mensaje de redención que el sacerdote daría.

Luisa había cosechado varias verduras selectas de su jardín y las había empacado cuidadosamente para darlas como ofrenda a la misión. Fue un gesto simple, pero uno que siempre honrarían.

Diego estaba feliz de pasar el día con su familia y descubrió que comenzó a relajarse e incluso empezó a ayudar a su madre y Luisa con algunas tareas en su pequeña casa.

Sin embargo, el lunes por la mañana llegó demasiado pronto, y regresó al trabajo, remolcando los enormes bloques de coquina a través de la bahía.

El día pasó muy rápido, mientras Diego hacía viaje tras viaje a través de la bahía; Primero remolcando los enormes bloques de coquina y luego, casi como para recompensar su esfuerzo, simplemente tiró de las balsas vacías de regreso a la isla Anastasia. Para ser cargado de nuevo.

Había colocado su equipo de pesca en el bote, y cuando había un descanso para almorzar, o cuando la siguiente balsa aún no estaba lista para remolcar, lanzaba su anzuelo a la bahía, con la esperanza de atrapar algo para la cena. Le había dicho a Luisa que bajara a la orilla temprano cada tarde y viera si tenía un trozo de tela verde colgando de un palo en la parte delantera de su bote. Si lo veía, esperaría en la orilla, tomaría la canasta con el pescado de la cena y regresaría a casa.

En su mayor parte, su sistema funcionó bien; La familia tendría pescado fresco para la cena o podría cambiarlo por pollo o cordero, y, al mismo tiempo, no gastaría ninguno de los salarios duramente ganados para comprarlo.

<h1 align="center">❧ 2 ❧</h1>

El trabajo cansaba a Diego, y al atardecer, cuando se dirigía a casa, solo deseaba una cena caliente y una buena noche de sueño. Por supuesto, necesitaba pasar algún tiempo tanto con Luisa como con su madre enferma. Había notado hace una semana que su madre tenía dificultades para respirar y necesitaba mantenerse caliente sentada junto al fuego de la cocina gran parte del día.

El miércoles, poco después de irse a trabajar, la respiración de su madre simplemente se detuvo. Ella se había ido.

Luisa estaba parada en la orilla, esperando que él remolcara la enorme balsa a través de la bahía para contarle de su fallecimiento.

Cuando Diego inclinó la cabeza y se cruzó, su mente volvió a los días posteriores a la muerte de su padre y de tantos otros habitantes del pueblo. Las lecciones aprendidas en ese momento, le enseñaron que era necesario enterrar el cuerpo bajo tierra lo antes posible. Sin embargo, necesitaba la aprobación y las bendiciones de un sacerdote.

Tomando la mano de Luisa, caminaron juntos a la pequeña capilla de Nuestra Señora de La Leche para encontrar al fraile y pedirle consejo e instrucciones.

Era demasiado tarde para tener el entierro, así que tuvieron que esperar a la mañana siguiente.

Como prometido por el fraile, un poco después de la primera luz de la mañana siguiente, cuatro hombres de la ciudad acompañaron al fraile a la casa de Diego. Colocaron el cuerpo en una simple caja de pino y se lo llevaron al cementerio.

Después de las oraciones del fraile, Diego y los cuatro hombres pusieron el ataúd en el suelo y comenzaron a cubrirlo con la tierra.

Luisa, triste por la pérdida de Diego, se quedó a su lado hasta que finalmente se fueron a casa. Se había dado cuenta de que ahora era ella quien debía tener el control de la casa, y no había nadie más a quien acudir en busca de consejo o guía.

Con ese pensamiento todavía en su mente, una patada en su vientre le recordó que pronto habría otra responsabilidad que ambos debían enfrentar.

A la mañana siguiente, Diego regresó al trabajo, nuevamente remolcando bloques de coquina a través de la bahía.

El trabajo en Castillo estaba avanzando, y Diego se sentía un poco orgulloso de sí mismo por ser parte, aunque solo una pequeña parte, del proyecto que ayudaría a proteger a su comunidad.

Cuando iba a la orilla, cada día, miraba a los soldados que manejaban el fuerte de madera justo al sur del nuevo sitio de construcción. Siempre parecían estar observando a los trabajadores en el fuerte y ocasionalmente practicando con disparos de cañón sobre la bahía.

Diego conocía a la mayoría de estos hombres, porque eran sus vecinos en la ciudad. Pasaban solo tres días a la semana en la empalizada, luego la mayoría de ellos también trabajaban en varias partes del proyecto de construcción cuando terminaban su tiempo de servicio.

Había una necesidad de que la economía de la ciudad prosperara, y, de maneras poco ortodoxas, lo hizo. No todas las transacciones involucraban dinero real; Gran parte de ella era un comercio de productos y servicios. Los valores de artículos específicos se establecieron con el tiempo, y los comerciantes sabían cuáles eran.

Había dinero en efectivo, por supuesto, y su valor era indiscutible. Aun así, la continua financiación poco confiable e impredecible de la Corona española hizo que el uso diario del artículo para el comercio de artículos fuera un respaldo confiable.

Diego, cuando se dio cuenta de que necesitaba mantener a su creciente familia cuidada, comenzó a pescar más cada día mientras remaba de un lado a otro de la bahía. Había descubierto que normalmente podía pescar tres o cuatro peces la mayoría de los días.

Ocasionalmente, había un día en que el clima no era favorable para remolcar coquina, y pasaba ese tiempo cazando en los bosques cercanos con el mosquete que había sido de su padre hace muchos años.

Un ciervo ocasional o un jabalí era un placer tanto para él como para Luisa.

Por la noche, mientras estaba sentado junto al fuego de la cocina, Diego se preocupaba por su familia y su futuro.

Sus pensamientos irían a lo que traería el mañana; ¿Más incertidumbre, más luchas o menos? ¿Qué habrá más allá de este momento, solo sueños, tal vez esperanzas?

Con la muerte de su madre todavía en su mente, miró a Luisa y pensó en el futuro nacimiento de su hijo. Lo lleva a un momento aleccionador; Pronto será padre. Es algo que nunca antes había considerado. Desde la edad de seis años, nunca supo lo que la guía de un padre podría significar para un niño.

Diego se aferra a su fe, agradecido por la fuerza de Dios para trabajar, aunque con una lucha constante y la voluntad de seguir adelante con la esperanza de "solo tal vez".

Sus pensamientos se desplazan hacia el presente, y comienza a cuestionar lo que estaba sucediendo a su alrededor. *"¿Se estaba construyendo el Castillo por amor al Rey y al país? ¿Era para España? ¿Era para el mejoramiento de la provincia y la protección de la gente, su gente, su familia, él mismo? ¿Quién es nuestro enemigo? ¿Qué los convierte en nuestro enemigo?"*

Esos pensamientos seguían formándose en su cabeza, y mientras cerraba los ojos y se preparaba para el trabajo del día siguiente, comenzó a preguntarse cuánto tiempo tomaría este proyecto y qué había en el futuro cuando estuviera completo.

Tal vez esos pensamientos eran una premonición de lo que estaba por venir, porque Diego descubrió, más tarde la semana siguiente, que los fondos de construcción, nuevamente, se habían agotado.

El rey Carlos II, en España, había desperdiciado mucho. Sin embargo, fue su madre, la reina regente Mariana, quien, cuando era niño, inicialmente proporcionó fondos para el Castillo y, aunque envejeció, todavía tenía cierta influencia sobre el rey.

El reconocimiento de que los fondos ya no estaban disponibles actualmente provino de los supervisores del edificio. Hablaron de retrasos en la financiación de España, con la esperanza de que volviera pronto.

Algo en la forma en que hablaban, llevan a Diego a comenzar a preguntarse qué debía hacer. No, lo que debe hacer. Su hogar, su esposa, su futuro hijo, su comunidad, eso debe ser lo primero.

Sabía que algunos de los trabajadores continuarían con el Castillo, y él ayudaría con él lo mejor que pudiera. Pero las otras cosas tenían que hacerse primero.

Comenzó a trabajar solo medio día, remolcando la coquina a través de la bahía y pasando el resto del día pescando para el apoyo de su familia. La mayoría de los otros hombres que habían estado trabajando en el Castillo encontraron trabajo en otros lares. Otros, como Diego, continuaron trabajando con la esperanza de que los fondos regresaran pronto.

Muchos hombres necesitaban encontrar otra forma de sobrevivir, por lo que el trabajo de construcción continuó disminuyendo nuevamente a medida que seguían yéndose.

Muchos de ellos necesitaban continuar sus vidas y se alejaron de San Agustín, a veces firmando a bordo de barcos que los llevarían a las áreas más desarrolladas del Caribe.

Los funcionarios del gobierno trataron de mantener las cosas en marcha, pero como antes, sin fondos confiables, la comunidad comenzó a reducirse y empobrecerse.

Diego era, al menos, pescador; y fue capaz de atrapar lo suficiente para intercambiar los artículos tan necesarios para su familia. Pero se había convertido en una existencia efímera de nuevo. Incluso los viajes dominicales a la iglesia, Luisa llevaba consigo ofrendas de verduras más pequeñas.

❧ 3 ❧

Diego recordó cuando tanto Luisa como él habían pasado gran parte de su adolescencia en el cuidado diario del fraile local.

Luisa, como hija única, y dos años menor que Diego y había perdido tanto a su padre como a su madre cuando su casa se derrumbó en un huracán hace ocho años. A la edad de doce años, fue acogida por los tíos ancianos de su madre.

Aunque la cuidaban y la mantenían, no eran sus padres, y nunca tuvieron hijos. Entonces, decidieron que la influencia de la iglesia sería lo mejor para su vida cotidiana.

Fray José Sánchez de la pequeña capilla de Nuestra Señora de La Leche era un hombre amable, y se dio cuenta de que había cosas que ella podía hacer ayudando con gran parte del cuidado diario de la capilla.

Fue casi al mismo tiempo que Diego, también un alma perdida, a los catorce años de edad, vino al fraile en busca de algún trabajo que pudiera hacer para ayudar a su madre. María había trabajado cosiendo y tejiendo mantas y ropa para mantener su existencia, pero le dejó poco tiempo a para Diego.

El fraile les dio a cada uno de ellos cosas que hacer que disminuirían su carga y, al mismo tiempo, ayudarían a la iglesia; pero también pensó que serían mejores católicos si les enseñaba a leer y escribir. Entonces, resolvió darle lecciones a cada uno de ellos tres veces por semana.

Durante los tiempos intermedios, Luisa fue puesta a trabajar desempolvando y limpiando la capilla, y Diego fue asignado como aprendiz de uno de los hombres locales con instrucciones de cuidar el bote plano de la iglesia y aprender a pescar.

Con el paso del tiempo, los cambios de salud fallidos descubrieron que Luisa era necesaria para ayudar y ayudar a cuidar al anciano Fraile. Aunque ayudaba en la capilla cuando podía, Diego ahora trabajaba como pescador a tiempo completo, con su propio bote plano que había construido, para mantenerse a sí mismo y a su madre.

Sin embargo, pasaba casi todo su tiempo libre en la misión, asegurándose de que se mantuviera el cuidado de su bote plano y que hubiera pescado fresco disponible. Además, le gustaba estar cerca de Luisa siempre que podía, y se sentaban juntos y leían muchas de las notas y libros que Fray Sánchez les había dejado.

Tanto Luisa como Diego descubrieron que había más recompensa por estar juntos, mientras estaban bajo el cuidado de la iglesia de lo que habían pensado al principio, y por lo general pasaban la mayor parte de su tiempo libre juntos.

Hace aproximadamente un año y medio, Diego fue a ver tanto al anciano fraile Sánchez como al tío abuelo de Luisa y se le concedió permiso para casarse con ella.

La madre de Diego, María, estaba feliz de ver a Diego y Luisa juntos, y ellos, los tres, trabajaron juntos para expandir la cabaña para acomodar a cada uno de ellos.

Era la primera vez en la vida adulta de Luisa que tenía una mujer que la guiaba en las tareas domésticas de una esposa. Después de años de luchar por ser madre y proveedora al mismo tiempo, María se alegró de tener a Luisa allí y también se encariñaba mucho con ella.

A medida que pasaba el primer año de su vida juntos, Diego se estaba volviendo cada vez más capaz de mantener a su nueva familia ampliada. Sin embargo, con la financiación poco confiable del Castillo y la reducción de los ingresos, necesitaba pasar más tiempo como pescador comercial.

Pudo capturar suficiente pescado durante la mayoría de los días para comerciar por los bienes necesarios e incluso para vender a varias tiendas locales.

Diego se había hecho consciente que debía mejorar la situación en la que se encontraba, para asegurar la seguridad de su familia. Muchos de sus vecinos se ~~en~~ encontraban en una situación similar.

Esta situación se estaba convirtiendo en un punto frecuente de discusión entre los hombres de su vecindario. Esos puntos se vieron exacerbados por las diferencias sociales que eran comunes en San Agustín y en todas las colonias españolas.

Diego, como muchos de sus vecinos, eran 'Criollos' (personas en su mayoría de descendencia española o europea, nacidas en el nuevo mundo) y aunque legalmente españoles, estaban socialmente clasificados por debajo de los funcionarios del gobierno y los de la autoridad de control de clase alta, que eran en su mayoría 'peninsulares' (personas nacidas en España).

Muchos de los vecinos de las clases bajas o 'Mulatos' (personas de raza mixta) tenían aún más dificultades para ganarse la vida decentemente, pero juntos eran parte de la comunidad. Sin embargo, era la iglesia católica la que proveía un terreno común, e hizo mucho para mantener las cosas unidas. Además, siempre hubo lealtad al Rey.

Diego y los otros hombres hablaban mucho y con frecuencia sobre el futuro, con la esperanza de que la construcción se convirtiera nuevamente en la principal fuente de ingresos para su comunidad.

4

Diego tenía solo dieciocho años cuando el gobernador Pablo de Hita y Salazar fue reemplazado por el gobernador Juan Márquez Cabrera.

El gobernador Cabrera era conocido por ser un poco abusivo con la población en general, y muchos de los habitantes, como Diego, estaban felices de evitar su atención siempre que fuera posible. Sin embargo, mantuvo el control, y había una sensación de seguridad bajo su mando.

Con el paso del tiempo y los acontecimientos recientes, Diego se estaba preocupando cada vez más; Y con el nacimiento de su hijo próximamente, se dio cuenta de que debía estar preparado para mantener a su familia y protegerlos también.

La seguridad se había convertido más en el punto de discusión entre los hombres de la ciudad, y todos habían encontrado la necesidad de entender quién era su enemigo potencial, y por qué.

Las discusiones sobre los británicos que habían ocupado y ahora fundado una ciudad costera a solo dos días de navegación, conocida como 'Charles Town' en la parte sur de las Carolinas, fue una de las principales razones decisivas para la construcción del Castillo de piedra.

La gente del pueblo sabía que los británicos habían estado luchando contra la Corona española durante años, y ahora esa lucha continuaba acercándose a la provincia, en la Nueva España. Aunque no todos entendían de qué se trataba la discusión, todos sabían que sus propias vidas y las de sus familias estaban en peligro si los británicos alguna vez llegaban.

También sabían que las flotas españolas usaban su puerto como la última parada de suministro en su camino de regreso a España, y que la existencia y la economía de la ciudad dependían de gran parte del comercio resultante.

Juntos, estos hombres, vecinos y amigos estaban cada vez más preocupados e incluso asustados. Muchos encontraron fuerza al unirse a los Soldado y al ejército español. En contraste, muchos otros juraron lealtad al Rey y, aunque originalmente fueron creados para aquellos de bajo estatus social, se unieron a la milicia local.

Fue allí donde Diego encontró su lugar. Podía continuar encontrando suministros y mantener a su familia, pero ser un miembro listo y capaz de defender su hogar y su ciudad.

Una semana más tarde, con la llegada de tres barcos españoles, rápidamente se corrió la voz de que se habían prometido fondos adicionales y que el trabajo en el Castillo podría reanudarse nuevamente.

Fue un regreso lento, una vez el trabajo en el Castillo comenzó de nuevo. Muchos de los trabajadores calificados habían encontrado otras fuentes de ingresos, y otros habían dejado San Agustín para trabajar en lugares lejanos. Pero el trabajo continuó, y con la ayuda de los indios nativos locales Timucua, Guale y Apalache, el progreso comenzaba a mostrarse.

Las dimensiones exteriores de la estructura estaban completas, y las gruesas paredes eran cada vez más altas. En su mayor parte, el muro había alcanzado casi su altura final prevista de veintisiete 'Pies' a lo largo de la costa oriental. Los bastiones para la artillería, ubicados en cada una de las cuatro esquinas, serían la parte más sustancial y consumirían una gran cantidad de coquina.

Aunque el progreso fue lento al principio, los trabajadores calificados comenzaron a regresar de Cuba y otras islas del Caribe. Incluso algunos convictos cubanos fueron traídos con ellos para proporcionar mano de obra adicional. Diego regresó al trabajo de tiempo completo de remolcar coquina a través de la bahía, pero había aprendido que la pesca todavía era necesaria a sus esfuerzos de proveer para su familia.

Diego quería mantener su obligación con la construcción del Castillo, pero también asegurarle a Luisa que siempre iba a estar allí para ella y su futuro hijo. Eso significaba que obtener un ingreso confiable seguía siendo el principal desafío.

Por lo tanto, pasaría todo el tiempo que pudiera pescando y remolcando coquina; Sin embargo, buscaba otras tareas que podría podía hacer para garantizar su seguridad. Descubrió que su habilidad en la construcción de botes planos era necesaria, y varias personas estaban buscando la reparación o el reemplazo de ellos.

Esto significo que su semana laboral se hiciera aún más larga mientras trataba de hacer todo lo que podía. Sin embargo, el domingo era el día de descanso del Señor. Tanto él como Luisa pasarían gran parte de ella en la misión, pero siempre juntos.

Irónicamente, la vista de Fraile Sánchez había estado fallando, y lo dejó con la incapacidad de leer el evangelio y los pasajes que tanto amaba. Por lo que, en esos domingos cuando Diego y Luisa podían pasar tiempo con el fraile, se turnaban para leerle los pasajes en voz alta mientras se sentaba en silencio y escuchaba con los ojos cerrados.

❧ 5 ❧

Los meses de verano pasaron lentamente, y Luisa se sintió más incómoda a medida que se acercaba el nacimiento del bebé. Los meses de verano eran frecuentemente calurosos, y cuando había poca o ninguna brisa, era difícil incluso moverse en su casa. A menudo le resultaba necesario mantener una toalla mojada o un gorro en la cabeza para mantenerse fresca, y sus movimientos se ralentizaron aún más lentos y limitados.

Diego estaba preocupado por ella e hizo todo lo posible para tratar de ayudar siempre que pudo. Pero esto era algo de lo que ninguno de los dos sabía nada ni tenían ninguna experiencia.

Luisa descubrió que cuando podía caminar hasta la ciudad, generalmente se sentía un poco mejor y podía obtener los artículos necesarios para el cuidado de su casa. En varios viajes a la ciudad, se detuvo en la tienda propiedad del Señor Riguez.

A fines de agosto, se detuvo para ver si podía comprar ~~unos~~ unas 'varas' de tela de algodón que, cuando estaba mojada, podía colgar en las ventanas de la casa, y la brisa de alguna manera enfriaría la casa a una condición más cómoda.

Aunque conocía al Señor Riguez, este día, él estaba ocupado en la parte trasera de su tienda, y una mujer mayor se acercó para ayudarla a encontrar lo que necesitaba. Fue su esposa quien casualmente estaba allí ese día. La señora Elana Riguez no pudo evitar ver que Luisa estaba embarazada y se acercaba mucho a su hora, así que hizo que Luisa se sentara y procedió a completar las compras necesarias para ella.

Elana Riguez había conocido a María Rivera y sabía que su hijo Diego estaba casado con Luisa. Pero no se había dado cuenta de que estaba embarazada. Le preguntó a Luisa quién estaba disponible para ayudarla durante el nacimiento de su hijo y se sorprendió al saber que Luisa, con la cabeza inclinada, dijo que no había nadie más que Diego para ayudarla.

Elana decidió en ese momento que se convertiría en la partera de Luisa cuando naciera el niño. Ella le indicó que le dijera a Diego que viniera a buscarla una vez estuviera cerca de dar a luz y que ella estaría allí desde el momento en que comenzara su trabajo de parto. Con emociones encontradas, Luisa estaba agradecida por la atención de la señora Ríguez y, sin embargo, se sintió culpable, al darse cuenta de que era necesario.

Diego pudo ver que Luisa estaba tratando de mantenerse al día con la casa y las tareas de cocinar y limpiar, pero no podía ocultar su incomodidad. Descubrió que su cuidado por Luisa era un sentimiento aún más fuerte de lo que pensaba y sabía que debía convertirse en una ayuda más en la casa.

El momento del nacimiento de su hijo estaba repentinamente sobre ellos cuando Luisa dejó escapar un grito de agonía a última hora de la noche del primer lunes de septiembre.

Luisa había seguido las instrucciones de la señora Ríguez para decírselo a Diego, y él fue de inmediato a buscarla. Fue una noche difícil, y no fue hasta casi el mediodía del día siguiente que nació su hijo.

Diego recibió instrucciones de permanecer fuera de la habitación mientras Luisa estaba de parto y, aunque no quería, siguió sus deseos incluso cuando escuchó a Luisa gritar o cuando el nuevo bebé lloró. Fue un alivio para él cuando la señora Riguez salió de la habitación con el bebé, envuelto en una toalla, en sus brazos. Ella le dijo que Luisa estaba bien y que ahora estaba descansando.

Con eso, le entregó el bebé cuidadosamente a Diego y le dijo, con una sonrisa: "Conoce a tu nueva hija Diego".

Diego tomó a la bebé y la sostuvo con cuidado mientras la miraba. ¡Una hija! Él y Luisa no habían pensado mucho en el sexo de su hijo, pero él había asumido que sería un niño. Ahora una avalancha de emociones se apoderó de él cuando se dio cuenta de que era el padre de una niña.

Sin preguntar, llevó a su hija a la habitación donde descansaba Luisa, le sonrió y le dijo: "Ella es hermosa, ¿cómo la llamaremos?"

Se sorprendió cuando ella le dijo: "Tu madre sabía que íbamos a tener un bebé, pero no llegó a verla, ¿podemos llamarla María en honor a tu madre?"

Diego guardó silencio durante varios momentos, y mirándola y luego a la señora Riguez dijo: "Hemos pasado por muchas cosas juntos, Luisa, y cuando se necesitaba y necesitábamos ayuda, de alguna manera esta siempre nos encontraba encontró. Creo que debemos estar agradecidos por aquellos que siempre estuvieron allí. Entonces, ¿estarás de acuerdo en que su nombre sea María Elana?"

A medida que comenzaba una nueva vida para la familia Rivera de Diego, Luisa y María Elana, la carga de trabajo de Diego iba a ser un poco más difícil, pero no se preocupó por eso. Luisa también tenía mucho más que hacer ahora, y aunque había vuelto a ser ella misma, el cuidado adicional necesario para María Elana era una carga para ella.

Diego estaba de vuelta remolcando coquina dos días después y estaba agradecido de que la señora Riguez pasara casi todos los días para ver cómo estaban Luisa y María Elana. El valor de la pequeña ciudad y los vecinos que vivían allí se volvieron más relevantes para ellos cada día.

EPÍLOGO

A finales del año 1684, la vida de Diego, Luisa y María Elana se había convertido en una rutina cotidiana; eso era lo que el ciudadano español promedio de San Agustín había llegado a vivir.

Había sido un año crucial para ambos. Juntos, Diego y Luisa habían visto cambios en sus vidas que incluían la muerte de la madre de Diego y la continuación de la construcción en el Castillo, después de un tiempo de financiación lenta.

Diego continuó usando sus habilidades para ayudar a en la construcción siempre que pudo. Había mejorado su capacidad para alimentar y cuidar de manera confiable a su familia, y aun así estar preparado para defenderlos.

Luisa también había aprendido mucho ese año. Al igual que Diego, había crecido sin la orientación típica que sus padres le hubieran podido proporcionarían proporcionar. La iglesia le había enseñado muchas cosas útiles, pero fue solo después de que ella y Diego se casaron que ella tuvo una madre para ayudarla a guiarla en las tareas domésticas típicas.

Con el nacimiento de María Elana, ambos se dieron cuenta de que ahora eran ellos los que proporcionaban el sentido y enfoque necesario. Aprendieron que los vecinos a menudo estaban disponibles cuando era necesario, y decidieron reciprocar a su comunidad siempre que fuera posible.

Dos años después del nacimiento de María Elana, Luisa dio a luz a un segundo hijo, un niño llamado José Pedro, llamado así por el fraile y padre de Diego. Resultó que María Elana, de dos años, era una buena hermana mayor para su hermano pequeño. Diego estaba feliz de tener un hijo que algún día pudiera trabajar con él.

Las lecciones que aprendieron de Fray Sánchez a medida que crecían los siguieron a lo largo de sus vidas. La iglesia siempre fue algo muy importante, y su fe en Dios nunca los abandonaría.

Era muy inusual que tanto Luisa como Diego pudieran leer y escribir, ya que era raro que alguien que no hubiera nacido de la aristocracia tuviera esa habilidad. Pero aun así mucho más inaudito para una mujer de pocos recursos, e incluso entonces, en el seno de la iglesia.

Pero a medida que María Elana y José Pedro crecían, Luisa decidió que no solo les transmitiría esa habilidad a ellos, sino que también comenzó a dar clases para varios otros niños pequeños de la ciudad.

A medida que pasaron los siguientes diez años, la ciudad de San Agustín continuó creciendo. Todavía hubo momentos en que las cosas se ralentizaron casi hasta detenerse, pero, de alguna manera, continuó prosperando.

A finales de 1695, el Castillo estaba completo, y la vieja fortaleza de madera en ruinas había desaparecido.

Diego continuó pescando y también se convirtió en un buen carpintero que podía construir botes planos para algunos de los otros hombres de la ciudad. A medida que José Pedro crecía, ayudaba a su padre a construir los barcos, pero su verdadero interés estaba en el cuidado de caballos y ganado.

A la edad de diez años, José Pedro se convirtió en un muchacho de establo en la cuadra central de la ciudad y se le dio la tarea de cuidar el caballo del gobernador, Laureano de Torres y Ayala.

Tres años más tarde, cuando el gobernador cambió de nuevo, José Pedro, un excelente jinete, se convirtió en un joven arriero para varios ranchos ganaderos en los alrededores y traería rebaños a San Agustín para el sacrificio.

María Elana también se convirtió en una valiosa ciudadana de su la ciudad. Para orgullo de su padre y su madre, se convirtió en una ayuda vital para la salud de sus vecinos y en una partera experimentada a la edad de diecisiete años.

La vida para Diego y Luisa era más segura a medida que pasaba el tiempo, y ambos encontraron paz al saber que sus hijos estaban preparados para el futuro.

Pero la amenaza interminable de invasión de los británicos, piratas o incluso otros, siempre estuvo ahí. Resultó ser cierto cuando, siete años después de la finalización del Castillo de San Marcos, en 1702, los británicos atacaron; y en vigor para tomar y ocupar la ciudad no mucho antes de la época navideña.

Fue con renovado temor que Diego y Luisa, junto con María Elana y José Pedro, fueron con casi mil quinientas personas del pueblo al nuevo Castillo, donde permanecerían durante cincuenta y un días.

Diego y José Pedro se unieron a los soldados en la el parapeto y el terraplén de armas en la lucha, mientras que Luisa y María Elana trabajaron incansablemente, ayudando a cuidar a quienes necesitaban ayuda.

Era una nueva generación de personas que ahora iban a tener la responsabilidad de proteger sus hogares, y tanto María Elana, de dieciocho años, como José Pedro, de dieciséis, estaban listos para unirse y retomar la tarea.

Cuando se levantó el asedio, después de casi dos meses, la familia regresó a su casa incendiada. Fue con lágrimas en los ojos, pero resueltos en sus corazones, que comenzaron a reconstruir de nuevo.

Author Biography

Richard B. Christie

Once he retired from the business world, a love for the reenactment of early American history just seemed to be a normal result. Of course, in Florida, the early Spanish period was what he would be involved with. He joined several groups in nearby Saint Augustine, the oldest continuously occupied city in North America.

Working as a volunteer reenactor, he found himself demonstrating and describing many of the historical actions and daily procedures of the 16th, through the 19th centuries, to the many visitors who came to see the town.

Biografía del autor

Una vez que se retiró del mundo de los negocios, el amor por recrear la historia temprana de Estados Unidos parecía ser un resultado normal. Por supuesto, en Florida, el período español temprano fue en el que estaría involucrado. Se unió a varios grupos en la cercana San Agustín, la ciudad más antigua ocupada continuamente en América del Norte.

Trabajando como recreador voluntario, se encontró demostrando y describiendo muchas de las acciones históricas y procedimientos cotidianos desde el siglo XVI asta el siglo XIX a los muchos visitantes que venían a ver la ciudad.